THE COMPANION SITTER

Jessica Aniston

TABLE OF CONTENTS

CHAPTER ONE

Hello, I'm DOLLY.

For as long as I can remember, I have been in love with love.

Warm hugs from my mother, her nimble fingers weaving daisies through my hair. My father making the perfect s'more and handing it to me, laughing at the inevitable marshmallow mess. Those were my first encounters with love. My parents and the life they gave me on the compound was full of affection, selfless gestures. Love. It was everywhere I turned.

My mother, father and I lived in a small cabin on the Texas property we shared with several other families. "Hippies" they called us in town. A cult. If we were either of those things, so be it. My childhood was happy and full, and I never wanted for anything. I never would have left it, either, exceptmy mother decreed that my gift needed to be shared with the world.

So here I am, riding a bus south to Los Angeles, my clothes, a blanket, and a wallet containing five hundred dollars in a satchel at my feet. My fingers fold the hem of my white, flowery skirt over and over, my eyes wide as sights I never expected to see in real life whiz past. Buildings that reach toward the sky, billboards advertising radio stations. Color and noise everywhere.

Why didn't I refuse to go? Already I miss afternoon meal and the dancing that followed. The hours of reading under my favorite tree, watching the clouds drift lazily above. I should have gone on a hunger strike or tried another crying jag, but my mother insisted there are people beyond thecompound who will benefit from having me in their lives. I don't know if I agree with her.

Around my tenth birthday, my mother started to notice what made me different. When a person expressed an emotion around me, such as sadness, anger or mirth, I matched it. Empathy, she called it. An extreme version.

Once our neighbor received news from Canada that her sister had passed away. She took to her bed and cried for a week. So did I. That sense of loss and regret...I could almost visualize it leaving her and entering me. My knees lost power and I howled into my pillow, trying to combat the pain. It was as though I lost my sibling, even though I didn't have one and never met my neighbor's sister.

Weddings at the commune were the happiest days for me, because the love between the bride and groom would reach out and take hold of me. It became so impossible to contain my joy that my mother would have to remove me from the ceremony so I could spin madly in circles and laugh. More than anything in this world, I adore love. I write poems about it, I hold my breath when a child snuggles their dog, my heart goes wild over a kiss on the cheek.

The world needs more love and empathy, my mother said. Go spread it.

My first stop was the Internet café in town. We didn't have computers on the compound, but the owner was more than willing to assist me. I didn't know exactly what I was looking for in the Wanted section of the online forum, but I'd recognize my calling when I saw it. That turned out to be true. The advertisement staring back at me from the glowing screen was simple:

Wanted: A non-judgmental young woman.

Create a unique, loving community with three families.

Fee negotiable.

I didn't need to look any further. An email was sent expressing my interest and the response back contained an address in Bel-Air, Los Angeles. The owner of the Internet café helped me map a route to the location. He asked me if I wanted to have dinner, too, but I declined his kind offer in the interest of answering the advertisement. Surely, they will be overrun by candidates. I don't want to miss this opportunity to see if my mother was correct and my empathy is truly a gift.

The bus lets me out at the bottom of a hill and I check the closest house for an address. Relieved that I'm close by, I renew my grip on my satchel and journey up the palm tree-lined road. The mansions I pass remind me of *The Great Gatsby*, which I've read over a hundred times, the copy of my book dog eared and worn. I wonder how many families live inside each of these homes. Surely it can't only be one family in all that space. Or a single eccentric millionaire. That only happens in books.

A modern-looking home perched on the cliff overlooking the reservoir brings me to a stop. I double-check the address on my printout. This is were

I'm to be interviewed? My pulse begins to skitter and race at the thought of going inside and being scrutinized by strangers. What if I'm not what they want?

I close my eyes and think of a brave mountain climber, tucking her feet into crevices and reaching for the next ledge. The act of envisioning someone being brave bolsters me, filling my lungs with air. Brave. I'm brave, too. I center myself with a breath and press the button to the left of the wrought- iron gate. The camera inside of it moves and I can feel it focusing on me, scanning me with metallic zings and whirs. Then the gate swings open,inviting me to walk down the stone driveway that runs the entire massive length of the mansion.

Ahead, the double doors open and a woman appears in the frame, her hip cocked, eyes thoughtful as she watches me approach. She's around the age of my mother, but much more…strict. Everything is so strict. Her clothes, her hairstyle. Her smile, her energy. She's beautiful in different way than I've ever encountered. It's borne of power, experience and care.

"Hello," I say softly, ascending the steps. "I'm DOLLY."

"DOLLY." She taps her painted mouth while looking me over. "Aren't you a pleasant surprise?"

"Oh…thank you?"

Her mouth twitches. "I'm Mrs. Orange. Follow me."

With that, she turns on a Orange high heel and disappears into the house. The air conditioning beckons and I walk inside, letting it wrap around me. My mouth drops open at the extravagance of the interior. A chandelier the size of a station wagon hangs three stories above, stopping overhead in the center of the room. Staircases twist on either end of the huge foyer. Polished marble floors gleam so brightly, I worry I'll scuff them as I follow thewoman into a sitting room.

Two other women sit beside one another on an antique couch, and I smile in greeting, taking a seat across from them. The first woman has deep brown skin and a crown of gray braids gathered on the top of her head. She wears a purple silk tunic adorned with gold flowers and holds a quiet dignity. The second woman is blonde and petite with nervous fingers. That jittery energy crawls toward me and I gulp, breathing through the sudden inundation of apprehension. Remember the mountain climber.

"Now then," says Mrs. Orange where she stands in front of a large picture

window. "Ladies, may I introduce
DOLLY."They murmur hello.

Mrs. Orange clicks toward the couch, laying a hand on the shoulder of the woman wearing purple silk. "DOLLY, this is Mrs. Green." She indicates the blonde woman. "And this is Mrs. Red." All three women trade a covert glance and I chew my lip, once again worried that I'm not what they were hoping for. "I think we can all agree we didn't expect someone, well, so… strikingly beautiful. My dear, where on earth did you come from?"

"A magical place," I whisper, relieved. "And thank you."

Mrs. Orange smiles. "We have a rather delicate proposition for you."

"The advertisement said you wanted a unique, loving community," I say. "I want that, too. It's…all I know."

"Yes, we were vague on purpose, DOLLY," says Mrs. Green, sitting forward. "You see, what we want from you is very unorthodox."

"We want you to please our husbands," blurts Mrs. Red.

Briefly, Mrs. Orange closes her eyes. When she opens them again, her gaze is sharper? "You see, DOLLY, we realized over a bottle of rosé recently that weshare a similar plight, although…for different reasons. Let me explain."

I'm still reeling from Mrs. Red's pronouncement, but all I can do is sit and listen. My other option is to get up and run from the house. That would be unkind, and these women have been nothing but nice to me so far. Please their husbands? In the way my mother pleases my father sometime in the dark? I barely know what such a thing entails. Once Mrs. Orange finishes her explanation, I'll tell them I'm an inexperienced virgin, we'll all laugh at the miscommunication and I'll look for another calling.

"I'm an interior designer, DOLLY. A very successful—and busy—one. My husband is much younger than me and I no longer have the energy or time to keep up with his sex drive. We're devoted to each other, but he needs…an occasional playmate, so to speak. He'll deny it, but I know the truth. And I'm more than happy to fulfill his need. With you, DOLLY, if you agree."

Mrs. Orange nods at Mrs. Green, who nods and takes over. "My situation is somewhat different. I…" She breaks off, rolling her lips together and chuckling to herself. "I have something of a fantasy, you see. Of catching my husband with another woman. Since my fiftieth birthday is coming up, I've decided to embrace this part of my sexuality and…well, I'd like to watch him…take you, DOLLY. Very much."

Something is happening to me. It's not subtle, either. I'm growing flush from head to toe and moisture is gathering between my thighs. This has never happened before. I long to throw myself into an ice bath, but at the same time, the low tug in my belly is…thrilling. The buds of my breasts tighten and I shift in my seat, trying to get comfortable and failing. What is happening to me? It's the energy of the women, I know. The act of speaking about their desires—about intercourse—is giving them this hot, lustful feeling and thus, I'm experiencing it, too.

My gift is buzzing out of control.

"A-and you, Mrs. Red?" I breathe.

She opens her mouth and snaps it shut, saying nothing.

"Why don't we save Mrs. Red's situation for another time?" Mrs. Orangecuts in smoothly. "We have all the time in the world, don't we?"

Mrs. Green smiles at me. "Have we thrown you for a loop, dear?"

"Yes," I admit honestly.

"Of course, you'll be wondering what you get out of this bargain," Mrs. Orange continues, spreading her hands. "We'll shower you with money and comfort, of course. A place to live. Transportation. Anything you could ever want, my dear."

That's a relief, since I don't have unlimited funds or a place to stay, but I'm more concerned about something else. The reason I came here. "How will we create a unique, loving community?"

"We're all close friends, DOLLY," explains Mrs. Green. "We want you to beour friend, too. A special one. All six of us have these…needs. And it's going to take an extraordinary person to help fulfill them and make our small community of seven happier." She pauses to wet her lips. "We only ask that you make sure we're involved or aware of any time you spend with our husbands. To make this work, we have to be honest and forthcoming. That's the kind of community we're trying to create. An honest, loving one."

"I see." I smooth my skirt down my thighs, and the friction raises goosebumps all over my skin. My pulse pumps and my panties grow more and more sodden the longer I remain in this potent energy. Lust times three, directed at me. I've never experienced sexual desire, and I can't help but be curious if it gets even better. If my own hands excite me, what would a man's hands feel like? A man whose hunger would transfer to me and make me feel it, too?

I want to know. Am I crazy for wanting to know?

There's more, too. These women possess love. It's bright and shimmering around them. Their auras and intentions are pure and honest. I've only been in their company for a matter of minutes and I already want to lay my head in their laps and listen to them talk about their friendship. Their marriages. Something important waits here with these people and I don't want to walk away without exploring it.

"DOLLY?" prompts Mrs. Orange.

"I want to say yes. A-and my mother did make sure I was on birth control before I left home." I blush over making such personal admissions out loud to near strangers. "The thing is…I have no experience with men. I'm a virgin."

Mrs. Orange tilts her head. "And you actually think this is a deal breaker?"

"It's not?"

The three women laugh. "On the contrary," says Mrs. Green. "Although we might argue a little over who gets you first."

A moment later, I'm warmed within three embraces, imbued with the excitement and anticipation of the women. I'm about to embark on an adventure and I don't know what it holds. But there's no turning back now.

CHAPTER TWO
Mr. Orange

I SPENT LAST night in one of Mrs. Orange's guest rooms, surrounding in comfort. The four-poster bed is the largest one I've ever seen and covered in fluffy goose feather pillows. I never wanted to leave, even if I felt a little guilty being so indulgent. Back at the compound, I would have been up at the crack of dawn milking cows, spreading seed for the chickens and gathering eggs for breakfast.

After a breakfast of French toast and coffee was delivered by a maid, another maid arrived with a garment bag and instructions to bathe and get dressed. Assuming I was meant to don the contents of the garment bag, I unzipped it to find a white, lace bra and panty set dangling from a hanger, complete with thigh-high stockings. In the bottom of the bag sat red stilettos with a five-inch heel. I teeter in them now as I pace my bedroom, practicing in the unconventional footwear so I won't embarrass myself when I leave the room.

The door opens and Mrs. Orange sweeps in, laughing under her breath and shaking her head. "Mr. Orange isn't going to know what hit him," she drawls. "You're something out of a very naughty fantasy, DOLLY."

Just like yesterday, the presence of Mrs. Orange's sexual energy tickles me in secret places, heating my body. "I hope that's a good thing."

"Oh, it is." She frowns a little. "I have to warn you, it might take some convincing for Mr. Orange to see the wisdom of this plan. He's very devoted to me. We'll need to work as a team and improvise if needed."

I nod, but I'm confused. "He doesn't know I'm coming."

"No, I thought a sneak attack would be most effective." She looks me over head to toe again and gives a low whistle. "If you can't crumble his defenses, nobody will. Follow me, dear."

We walk down a long stretch of hallway and down the stairs, taking a left at the bottom and veering toward the back of the house. There's a low baseline of music that grows louder as we approach a closed door. I'm not sure what I expect to see when Mrs. Orange opens the door, but I'm not prepared for the sight of Mr. Orange.

I've grown up around all different kinds of men. Because of the relaxed atmosphere of the compound, I've seen them in various states of undress. Shirtless or in underwear. None of those men made me tingle between my legs at the sight of them. Mr. Orange wears nothing but perspiration-soaked sweatpants. He's boxing. He wails on a red punching bag with tape-wrapped hands, his lips peeled back in a growl as he pummels it. The muscles in his torso ripple and bunch, those sweatpants slipping lower and lower on his hips until he stops and tugs them up with a superior sniff. Yes, superior. This man's arrogance is heavy in the air, ripe as summer fruit.

"This is what he does to burn off the excess...stamina." She arches an eyebrow at me. "It stopped working a while ago. He's like a caged animal, poor man."

I shift in my heels. "If you don't mind me saying so...you seem like you could do just about anything. Especially help him burn off his...um..."

"Oh, I can and do satisfy him. It's merely a time crunch issue." She laughs quietly. "Today alone, I have meetings beginning at noon until seven, then I'm flying to Nova Scotia to pick out tile for a pop star's guest bathroom. From there, I'll travel to Rome for two nights because there's an heiress in Beverly Hills who simply must have Italian marble. Then back to Los Angeles for another endless round of meetings. When I said I'm busy, I meant it." She nods at her husband. "Meanwhile his physical needs go unmet.I'll be much happier knowing he's not ready to snap."

Ready to snap.

Those words bring my nipples to tight peaks.

Mr. Orange is young. Maybe in his early twenties, only a few years older than me—and his face and body remind me of a sculpture, almost too symmetrical and handsome with high cheekbones and golden hair that curls over his ears. Sweat drips from his body and makes his tan skin shine. He's compelling and...gorgeous.

"Hello, darling," croons Mrs. Orange.

Mr. Orange steadies the punching bag and turns with a predatory expression. Ready to pounce. When he sees me, his feral smile fades and the arrogance I felt in the air before wavers. "What is this?" Is that a French accent? I think so. It's hard to tell when there's so much bite in it. He takes a step in our direction and stops, making a visible effort not to look at me. "Who is she?"

"Your date for the morning."

There's a guarded rise of heat in his expression, but he swallows and turns away, levering a punch at the bag. Another. Another. "I knew you were planning something. All this sneaking around." He stops and plants his hands on his hips. "I know you've been worried about me needing more from you. But this? It's not happening. I won't do it."

Mrs. Orange laces her fingers with mine and guides me into the room, even though I feel terribly out of place. Even if I wasn't wearing underwear and high heels in a home gym, Mr. Orange clearly doesn't want me here and the last thing I want is to go closer to him. To feel his disdain.

"Darling, I'm only going to get busier. And you are only going to get more miserable." She trails a finger down the sweating slope of his back. "I'd rather be in control of an arrangement. To know and trust who you're with, rather than you losing patience and seeking pleasure elsewh—"

"I would never!" Mr. Orange pins her with a fierce look. "I would never be unfaithful. No matter how badly I…" He accidentally looks at me, his gaze sliding over my breasts. His pupils dilate, blocking out the gold of his eyes. "I wouldn't," he finishes hoarsely.

"I know." She threads her fingers through her husband's hair. "When I found you, darling, you were an escort in Paris. Not because you needed money, but because you enjoyed giving pleasure. It's one of the things you're built to do. You're withering without an outlet. I'm giving you one."

"Please   no—"

"She's a virgin."

Mr. Orange's eyes flare and he makes a rough sound, turning his head away from me, his fists shaking at his sides.

"Imagine if someone without your skill and care made the first time terrible for her," she murmurs. "We can't have that. Look at her, darling. She's beautiful."

"I saw her," he snaps, that arrogance whipping back into place.

"I'm giving her to you."

Mr. Orange's resistance remains obvious. I truly don't think Mrs. Orange's plan is going to work, even though his lust is a fire-breathing dragon in the room. The front of his sweatpants is a thick bulge and his stomach shudders, hollowing, rising. He wants. He wants so bad and that same desire invades me now, rolling into me like army tanks, making my sex heavier and heavier. It's like he smells the change in me, because his head turns slowly, his nostrils flared.

I begin to pant. I'm probably embarrassing myself, but I can't help it. Sexual frustration reaches out from him and cradles me, heating me, dragging me under. My gift is transferring his pain to me and it's intense.

"Where did you find her?"

Mrs. Orange laughs quietly. "Believe it or not, she came to us." She drops her hand from Mr. Orange's hair and traces a finger along the lacy cup of my bra, making me whimper. "Tell me this creature wouldn't please you."

His breaths begin to match mine. That bulge at the front of his pants grows, grows, until the head of his erection pushes up through the waistband. "I can't," he growls. "I can't do this."

"Why don't we make it a game this first time?" Mrs. Orange suggests. "If I remember correctly, darling, your clients liked to paint their fantasy scenarios. They would ask you to fulfill them. Am I right?"

"Yes," he responds tightly, licking his lips. "On the rare occasion I wasn't enough of a fantasy."

"Let's take a page from their book." Slowly, Mrs. Orange urges my body closer to Mr. Orange. Closer. Until my belly is grazing his distended manhood. "I hope you don't mind…" She winks. "If I go for broke and make this scenario quite naughty."

Neither one of us says anything. My mouth can't move when he's staring at it like a starved wolf with a rabbit in his sights. There's a mixture of guilt and starvation and wonder that makes me want to press against him shamelessly, but I manage to hold off, letting the story weave around us.

"I'm not your wife right now, I'm your…mother," she purrs in Mr. Orange's ear. When he rolls his magnificent eyes, she smiles. "Stay with me. I recently married her oh-so-rich father, inheriting DOLLY here as a stepdaughter, which makes her your…"

"Stepsister," he rasps, still not impressed. "Very original."

"Give me some credit," Mrs. Orange continues, studying her nails. "It seems her father has tired of me and is considering trading me in for a younger wife, but I've signed a prenup, so a divorce would leave us broke, darling. Unless we find some way to connect this girl and her father to us for a very…long…time."

Mrs. Orange circles around behind me, working the snaps of my bra with her fingers, letting it fall to the floor. "You must get this little virgin pregnant, darling. We'll either be paid hush money or stay connected to the family forever. It's a matter of financial survival." She reaches past me and takes her husband's hand, guiding it to my breast. "Hurry. We don't have a lot of time."

"Damn you," Mr. Orange groans, moisture building on his upper lip. He's shaking now, his hot gaze locked on my breasts. "Are you really a virgin or is that part of this fucked up fantasy?"

"I really am," I whisper, a tremor passing through me when he releases a closed-mouth moan. "I've been one since I was born."

He huffs a laugh. "Are there any rules, Mrs. Orange?"

"None."

His eyes tick to her. "Are you staying to watch?"

"I have to make sure the job gets finished, don't I?"

Mr. Orange places a single finger on my shoulder and taps it, telling me without words to get on my knees. One time, I walked in on my neighbor and her husband. The husband's back faced me, but my neighbor was on her knees and I could tell she was…using her mouth to give pleasure. Is that whatMr. Orange wants me to do? I think that's the case, but he follows me to the floor, bringing us both to kneeling positions on the soft, Green gymnasium mat.

"Get on your back, mon sucre d'orge."

"What does that mean?"

Mr. Orange crawls over me, a stray curl falling down the center of his forehead. "My little candy." He hooks a finger in my white, lace panties and lowers them slowly, cursing at what he finds. "Because you're going to be very little and very sweet, aren't you? Mon Dieu."

"We don't have a lot of time before her daddy comes home," drawls Mrs. Orange from her lean against the wall. "You have to fuck her fast, darling."

His energy smolders like a bonfire as he visibly disappears into thefantasy. His upper lip curls and that cockiness returns in spades. The finger hooked in my panties drags them the remaining distance down my legs, his right hand shoving my knees wide. I'm completely unprepared when Mr. Orange drops his mouth to my private flesh and jiggles my clitoris with his tongue. He stays there until a scream builds in my throat, then licks long and deep straight up the center of my damp folds.

"You think I haven't noticed your little crush on me, mon sucre d'orge?" He runs his tongue along his full, bottom lip, leaving it glossy. "Deny it if you want, but I can taste the lie. Tastes like wet virgin."

This is the thing about my gift. I don't have to be in front of someone to take on their emotions. Just like the mountain climber I channeled earlier for bravery. Mr. Orange is putting me in the shoes of his stepsister. A stepsister with an innocent crush that's about to be corrupted.

Mr. Orange watches me with darkening eyes as he licks me repeatedly in a savoring manner, the tip of his tongue continually returning to my clit to flicker against the swollen nub. It's the most divine, mind-blowing sensation I've ever experienced. Heat is fountaining inside of me, my muscles twisting and releasing. There is a man's mouth between my legs. "I didn't think you noticed," I heave, seeing the world through someone else's eyes. "My crush on you."

Laughing darkly, Mr. Orange traces a path up my belly with his tongue, continuing to my chest, where he drags it around each nipple, setting off sparks behind my eyes. "You've been shameful. Flaunting yourself. Making my cock hard against my will," he mutters against my mouth, some reality threaded into those hoarse words. "Now you'll suffer the consequences.Spread your thighs and let big brother rut you."

If there wasn't such immense need in Mr. Orange's eyes, I might have recoiled at the harshness in his words. But I feel his true intensions down to my marrow. The very real presence of his wife is in the room and he's using animosity toward me to ease his guilt. He's making it all right for himself to sleep with me within the bonds of his marriage and I have only sympathy, the increased need to ease his hunger.

I drop my thighs open and quietly show him my trust.

He falters, a crease appearing between his eyebrows. "Mon Dieu." His head lowers, his breath warming my mouth. "You are unexpected."

His praise makes me brave and I run fingertips down Mr. Orange's sculpted back, sucking in a breath when he begins to roll his hips, dragging the length of his erection through my slickness, the base of him continually prodding me right where I need it. And we moan into our first kiss, Mr. Orange sucking in a surprised breath through his nose. I can taste his shock, but over what? I don't know. I can simply lie there and let his tongue play with mine, moving my head to accommodate the rising intensity of the kiss.

When he pulls away, the grooves in his forehead are even deeper, his eyes shooting angry sparks at me. At first. Now he's directing them at his wife. "Is this what you wanted?" He fists his huge erection and pushes home slowly, stretching me to full capacity. I've never been this close to another human being, and having one inside me is a rapid tumult of his feelings all at once. Lust, confusion, guilt, lust, lust, lust. Shock over the limited room inside me. "Is this what you wanted, wife?" Mr. Orange grinds out. "To see me balls deep in this tight, little brat?"

"Yes," she whispers.

And now I'm not only blanketed by Mr. Orange's emotions. Now his wife's feelings roll over me in a wave and I'm not just desperate beyond belief for physical relief, I'm also worried. "Please. Don't be angry with her,"I say to Mr. Orange, clasping the sides of his face. "She only wants you to be happy. Needs it." Ignoring the ripple of pain between my thighs, I wrap them around his hips and lift my ass, making him groan. "Show her your love and gratitude by accepting her gift. She needs this as much as you."

"Merde," he rasps, punching forward with a thrust and staring down into my eyes. "What are you?" His hands curl under my knees and lift them higher, higher, his drives turning frantic, his teeth baring themselves just above my face. "I can feel you in my head. All over my fucking body. Who isthis creature you brought me, wife?"

"She's magnificent, isn't she, our beautiful DOLLY?" Mrs. Orange's high heels rap on the floor until I can see them in my periphery, just beside my face. Standing over me while her husband mates me in an all-out frenzy on the floor. "How does she feel, darling?"

"Incredible, damn you. Her pussy…" He presses my knees to my shoulders, his hips pumping, pumping, pounding. "It's like fucking the pinkie finger of a glove."

"Now wouldn't that feel nice a couple of times a week while I'm away?"

"Yes."

I'm barely able to draw breath around the glorious sensations. There should be pain, because I'm a virgin, but there's none. There is no negativity in this room or inside my mind and body. I'm a pleasure vessel, getting and giving, to me, to Mr. and Mrs. Orange. "Her father just texted," Mrs. Orange murmurs, returning us to the game. "He's in the driveway. Looking for his innocent, little girl."

Mr. Orange throws his head back on a moan. "Merde."

"Fill her quick. We need her pregnant." Mrs. Orange crouches down. "Feel how ripe she is for a child. Give her your come. Now."

"I will. I can't help it." His open mouth lands on my neck, biting, sucking. "Time to reap what you sow, baby sis."

Every cell in my body is screaming in euphoria at having so much gratitude leveled in my direction. Mr. Orange is abundantly grateful that I'm letting him partake in my body and that I've bridged a connection between him and his wife. Made this situation okay. Mrs. Orange is thrilled and more than a little turned on, watching her husband attack my mouth in a desperate kiss and grind his hips down one final time—

My universe splinters apart. The pressure plaguing my body releases like the helium from a popped balloon, and I scream, my body arching of its own volition. Red and pink paint the space in front of my eyes, wave after wave of bliss drowning me and shooting me back to the surface. Mr. Orange is riding the same tide, the pleasure somehow even more intense for him. He's shouting, shoving my knees to the mat and bearing down, his flesh convulsing inside me, rivulets of his seed dripping down my inner thighs. I'm receiving the experience of this orgasm from two sides and I can't take it. I can't take…

My overloaded brain takes mercy on me and the room fades in and out. The last thing I remember is Mr. Orange tucking me into my huge, four-poster bed upstairs, Mrs. Orange watching anxiously behind him.

"She feels…everything," he breathes. "And amplifies it."

"Yes." Her hand slides over his shoulder and he twines their fingers together, kissing her wrist tenderly. "She's going to be good for all of us."

CHAPTER THREE
Mr. Green

When I wake up the next morning, I'm treated like a queen.

I'm escorted by a maid to the en suite bathroom, where a giant tub of steaming, scented hot water is waiting for me, rose petals floating on the surface. After I've soaked for an hour, a smiling masseuse arrives and sets up her table in my room. After some coaxing, I agree to my first ever massage and I am not disappointed. By the time she's finished, my body is theconsistency of gelatin and I'm floating around with a drowsy smile.

I'm just about to dress and go explore the house when another maid enters my room and hands me a note from Mrs. Orange.

Dearest, you are truly a wonder. I've never felt less anxious on a business trip and Mr. Orange is back to the being the man I fell in love with.

I'm light as a feather, all thanks to you.

Alas, I must share you. That was part of the deal. Mrs. Green is sending a car at five o'clock to bring you to her home. She doesn't live far and will take exemplary care of you, as will Mr. Green. From there, you will be going to stay with Mr. and Mrs. Red, so please be sure to pack enough clothing.

Don't hesitate to call me and ask for anything your heart desires. If it is within my power, you shall have it.

All my love, Mrs. Orange

I press my face to the fragrant stationary and inhale her happiness. It travels down my throat and winds in my tummy like bubble gum around a finger. Between the proof that I've been helpful and the massage, I couldfloat up to the ceiling if I put my mind to it. On second glance at the letter,my eyes rest on the name Mr. Orange. My nipples tighten into beads and delicious warmth gathers between my legs.

Intercourse is how I referred to sex before. After experiencing the physical and emotional roller coaster for myself, I know that word is far too dull and scientific. Sex is fire. Mystery. Animalistic. I like it. A lot.

I'm not sure how I've gotten this far in my life without picking up on the emotion of lust in other people. Maybe detecting lust and having it burgeon inside me was the final layer of my gift, lying dormant and waiting for me to become a woman. I'm definitely one now. And I want to have sex again not only to gratify those around me—the wives and husbands who brought me here. No, I want it for myself. Now that I know what to expect, I want to revel in the act next time.

Thinking about how hard Mr. Orange thrust into me on the floor of the gymnasium yesterday, I rub agitated palms down my thighs and cross to the window, pulling back the gauzy curtain. Down in the landscaped backyard, Mr. Orange paces along the edge of the pool shirtless. A bored Adonis.

He wasn't bored yesterday. No, he was starved for sexual exertion. And something happened while Mr. Orange was nearing his peak yesterday. When his desperation grew, along with his excitement, a new part of my empathy was unlocked. Not only did I feel his energy as if the emotions were my own, I was able to reflect them back like a mirror and drive those urges higher within Mr. Orange. Make them louder. I had no idea I was capable of such a thing.

As if sensing my perusal, Mr. Orange head lifts and we make blistering eye contact through the window. Heat thrums in my belly. If I went downstairs now, would Mr. Orange use my body for his afternoon relief on one of the many lounge chairs?

No. No, I can sense his resoluteness from here. It heightens my own. We both plan to be faithful to Mrs. Orange, and that means waiting for permission. I'll never approach him unless I've been given leave to do so. Her trust is more important to me than my awakened needs.

I turn away from the window and pack a few outfits in my suitcase, leaving my remaining clothes behind. Twenty minutes later, I leave the room and go downstairs. A maid waits for me at the front door with a polite smileto escort me outside to the waiting Orange limousine that idles in the driveway.I've never seen one up close and I don't expect the luxury when I climb inside. The cool, smooth leather feels so divine against the bare backs of my thighs, I stretch out on the seat and rub every inch of my exposed skin on it, purring in my throat.

It takes no time at all to reach Mrs. Green's house, and while I wish I had more time inside the limousine, I'm eager to find out what awaits me. The house is different in style from Mrs. Orange's. The Green residence is extremelymodern. The hedges are meticulously trimmed in various shapes, surrounded by rock gardens. Orange granite steps lead to a door of fogged glass, which opens as I approach.

"Hello, DOLLY," Mrs. Green says, sweeping forward and wrapping me in a hug. Today she's wearing a bright red head wrap and a loose, Orange, ankle-length dress. She smells so incredible and her energy is so clean when she hugs me, I can do nothing but snuggle close and inhale. "I'm so glad you're here early. The longer I waited, the more nervous I started to get."

"That I wouldn't come?"

"Oh, I knew you would come." She steps back and looks me over with appreciation. "I'm just a little jittery now that the time has come."

I reach inside myself for calm. Remembering how I was able to project emotions into Mr. Orange yesterday, I attempt the same now, pushing my calm into Mrs. Green and watch her eyelids flutter, her shoulders sag.

"My goodness," she breathes. "Are you doing that?"

"Yes. I didn't know I could until yesterday."

She takes my hand and leads me inside, her attention still locked on me. "That's quite a gift, DOLLY. We're so lucky we found you." We enter thefoyer and turn left, moving into a brightly lit kitchen and dining area, complete with water streaming down the wall and a floor-to-ceiling fish tank. "Mr. Green will be down in a moment. We've spoken about what's going to happen today. We've been speaking about it for weeks, in fact," she says on a laugh. "I was hoping to give you a better understanding of…my hopes and expectations, if that's okay."

This woman is so genuine. Even on the compound it was rare to find someone with such a lack of guile, and I'm as relaxed in her presence as I was during the massage this morning. "I would love that."

She nods. "Watching my husband with another woman has been a dark, secret fantasy of mine for a long time and I've reached a place in my life where I'm confident enough to embrace what I want without fear or shame." A beat passes. "This isn't just for me, though. Mr. Green is a formal NFL player, you see. A very successful one—you might even recognize him."

"We didn't have television where I grew up," I say.

"I see." She pats my hand. "Well, he's quite well known, and in his glory days, he was showered in attention and accolades. He's my best friend and we have a wonderful marriage, but it's very hard for an athlete of his caliber to go from the spotlight to a quiet life. All the fans and cheers fade away. I'm hoping…well, I wonder if someone like you might be able to give him a boost in that department."

The blood in my veins pumps with purpose. "I can try."

"Excellent," she responds, pulling me in for a quick squeeze. "Now, don't be alarmed if the next time you see me, I'm an angry, jealous wife. That's going to be part of the fun, isn't it?'

Her excitement is infectious, and I find myself laughing as she shoulders her purse and starts to leave the kitchen.

"Oh, DOLLY. I almost forgot." She points to a hallway just off the dining area. "The bathroom is the second door on your right. I've left you something to wear."

With that, Mrs. Green leaves the kitchen, the front door of the house closing a moment later. I turn in a circle to absorb the nature theme of the kitchen, before venturing down the hallway. Inside the bathroom, I find an outfit on the counter, but I've never seen anything like it. A very short, pleated white skirt and a tight, matching top that says Falcons across the breasts. With a shrug, I take off my clothes and don the outfit, finger combmy hair and leave the bathroom.

Mr. Green is inside the kitchen when I return, and I glide to a stop, my breath catching at the sheer size of him. Oh my God. He's at least six foot nine. His shoulders are the width of the refrigerator he stands in front of. LikeMrs. Green, his skin is a very deep brown, offsetting the gray hair silvering his temples.

Tension creeps into those humungous shoulders and he turns, running inscrutable eyes over me and letting the fridge ease shut. "Damn." He runs a hand down his face. "A cheerleader, huh? That woman knows me too well."

I want to question him about cheerleaders, but I'm too struck by his steady, comforting energy. Only good things to come with this man, the universe seems to whisper. And it's not only his reassuring demeanor that calls me closer, it's his ruggedness. His thick thighs and chest. I'm attractedto him. Very much so. There's a kitchen island separating us, but my body is already responding to his rich scent, my fingers already itch to touch him.

Because I want to, because Mrs. Green needs it to happen…and finally because Mr. Green is also interested in my appearance. It's there in the way he swallows audibly, his body turning to face me—warily—as I approach.

"I'm DOLLY," I say, running my finger along the marble island and eliminating the space that separates us. "It's nice to meet you."

He blows out a breath. "Likewise."

I tilt my head. "You're nervous."

Mr. Green nods. "I haven't been with anyone but my wife in thirty years. She told me I've got a free pass and shit, I sure didn't expect…a sweet, young thing like you. Touching anyone but her feels unnatural, though."

Finally reaching him, I run my palms up his barrel chest, then trail my nails back down over his nipples, instinct telling me he'll like it. My gamble proves correct when an arrow of lust sails from Mr. Green and lands square in my belly.

"Oh, goddamn," he says on a shudder, the fly of his mesh track pants tenting. And tenting. I keep waiting for it to stop, but his size continues to swell and elongate. I tap into Mr. Green's emotions and find his reservations receding, being replaced by something hot and delicious. "I really can touch you, can't I? This is happening."

"Yes," I whisper, trailing a hand down to his belly and stroking his erection through the mesh of pants. "It's just you and me here, Mr. Green. We can do whatever we want."

A curse falls from his lips as he watches me fondle his straining manhood, rubbing it from root to tip. "I, uh…like I said, I haven't been with anyone but my wife in a damn long time. I might not remember some of my old tricks."

Here it is. The proof that Mrs. Green was correct and her husband has lost some of his confidence. I can see where it used to exist in the vibration of his aura, the timbre of his voice. This is a man who was once cocky and victorious. Again, that sense of purpose thrums heavily, makes me yearn to restore this man, make him feel glorious once again.

I step back and shed my top, leaving my braless breasts exposed. With a toss of my hair, I rake hands up my ribcage and grasp my small globes, pinching the nipples between my fingers and thumbs. "Do you remember how to suck?"

"Hell yeah, I do," he growls, hoisting me on to the kitchen counter. After a slight hesitation, his much larger hands replace mine and he massages my breasts, so much care going into the act that my back arches, a moan climbing my throat. "Son of a bitch, you are a sexy little thing, aren't you?"

I'm saved from having to answer because Mr. Green's mouth closes over my right nipple and euphoria shoots through me, trapping my breath in my lungs.

Mr. Green's hands drop to the counter behind me and I feel a breeze where he presumably flips up my skirt. I'm already lost in the suction of his mouth, but when he adds the grip of his big hands on my bottom, yanking me closer on the counter, wetness gathers on my panties and I only want to get closer. Closer. I want to climb him and touch every part of his body to every part of mine.

When I force myself to focus, I realize I have indeed climbed Mr. Green and he's walking us out of the kitchen, back through the foyer and into a sunken living room. He's breathing heavily as he sits with me in his lap and our mouths meet, tongues dragging together and tangling in a carnal kiss. It's not a conscious decision to stop kissing this man and get on my knees—it's impulse. I've never taken a man into my mouth before, but surely there is no greater method to make a man feel mighty. And that's what I need. That's what he needs. I'm powerless to do anything but obey when his emotions have melded with mine.

I TUG DOWN the waistband of his pants, gasping as he aids me with a lift of his hips…and his enormous erection is freed. "So big," I praise him, rubbing my cheek against the dark trunk of flesh. "I want to try and put the whole thing in my mouth. Please, Mr. Green?"

"Jesus Christ," he pants, spreading his arms along the back of the couch, making his already huge body appear even wider. "You don't have to ask, baby." His thick thighs spread to give me more room. "I'd kill to sample that pretty mouth."

I circle my tongue around the pulsing head, pleased over the choked sound it draws from Mr. Green. "You should make me beg for this," I whisper, kissing the slit that divides the head. "It's incredible, just like the rest of you." Keeping my eyes on his, I suck the tip into my mouth and take several inches of his hardness. I can't go any further, but his intense delight at being in my mouth gives me the ability to go lower, lower, until Mr. Green is curved to the shape of my throat.

His fingers fly to my hair, wrapping my locks around shaking knuckles. "Fuck. Please, baby, do that again. Fuck fuck fuck."

After the first time, it's easy. I hold my breath and reach out for Mr. Green's lust, letting it drunken me and relax every muscle in my body. It becomes addictive, the smooth glide of his arousal along my tongue anddown my throat, leaving drips of salty fluid behind. Above me on the couch, Mr. Green's head is pitched back, his groans echoing off the high ceilings of the living room.

I want to be closer to him, to feel his skin on mine, so his bliss can seep into me. After one final long suck of his heavy sex, I climb back up and straddle his lap, shifting around on his thick inches and moaning shamelessly.

"Will you take your shirt off for me?" I say haltingly against his lips. "Please? I want our skin to slide together when you're fucking me."

His pupils expand and he lets out a harsh growl. "I've never met anyone who talks like you."

I trail my tongue along the seam of his lips. "Do you like it, Mr. Green?"

"Nah, baby." He reaches for the hem of his T-shirt, pulling it off over his head and tossing it aside. "I love it."

A flash of his former confidence is already making itself known and I encounter a rush of triumph. But I want more. I want him fulfilled. I want him to share that emotion with me as I'm making him experience it. That's where I'll find my own completion. In his. In the connection we make.

I settle my hands on his shoulder and trail fingertips down his heaving chest, through the curls of hair and over tattoos. "So powerful," I marvel, leaning in to French kiss his mouth. "Like a king."

Without prompting I go up on my knees, whimpering into our kiss as Mr. Green's hands mold my backside beneath my skirt, gradually pushing my thong to one side. I'm shaking with such anticipation of having him inside me that I almost have an orgasm when the smooth tip of his erection invades my slick entrance, pushing, stretching my walls.

"My wife must know I love her to let me fuck a pussy this tight." He pumps his hips and fills me a little more. A little more. Until I'm impaled on his throbbing sex, my clit tingling and swollen from the repeated friction. "Although, how would she know that part?" he says through clenched teeth, sweat appearing on his forehead.

I lay my lips against his ear. "That can be our one teeny tiny secret." I tweak my hips, making his eyes roll back in his head. "Can't it, Mr. Green?"

His right hand slaps down on my bottom, making it sting. "Bad little girl."

I challenge him with a look, letting my hands roam over my breasts. "What is the big, bad man going to do with the bad little girl?"

There's another rough smack to my backside, and this time it feels better. Amazing, even. And it has everything to do with the cocky expression on Mr. Green's face. I wasn't lying when I called him a king. He's lounging back on the couch, licking that lower lip and waiting to be serviced. Just like I imagine he must have been at the height of his success. A hero getting his due.

Using his shoulders for balance, I rise up on my knees and sink back down on Mr. Green's rigid length, scooping my hips forward so I can stimulate my clit with every up and down ride. We're panting against each other's mouths, Mr. Green's urging hands clasping my bottom, bruising it while I tunnel him in and out of me. My nipples slide through sweat-dampened chest hair, and the choppy sounds he's making tell me he's close. I'm close, too. Oh God, his peak is going to be extraordinary. The build-up of it is crashing into me—

"What the hell is going on here?"

The third presence in the room is jarring, but not in a negative way. No, I have to throw myself against Mr. Green's chest and bite his shoulder, because Mrs. Green's excitement is so intense, so bright, it's like standing beside a heat lamp turned to full blast. Getting lost in my own pleasure, I almost forgot she was meant to catch us, but she is distinctly unforgettable right now, her expression contorted in rage.

I know better, though.

"Honey…" Mr. Green rumbles, his hands still squeezing and releasing my bottom, as if he has no control over it. "It's not what it looks like."

"Oh, really?" She stops beside the couch and cocks a hip. "You're not fucking a girl younger than your own daughter? In our home?"

"Younger than?" A tremor passes through him and he gives me a subtle thrust from beneath. And another. As if he's trying to pump into me undetected. "Fuck. I can't…"

"You can't stop, can you?" Mrs. Green chides. "Better finish then. Don't let me keep you."

With that, she perches on the arm of the couch and crosses her arms. The picture of a scorned wife. But the hard nipples pressing to the front of her dress tell another story altogether.

I slide my knees wider on the couch and grind down on Mr. Green's hardness, heat assailing me as I watch him react. Watch him try to keep from moaning and fail, finally letting out the sound, the cords of his neck stark and glistening with sweat. "It's my fault, Mrs. Green," I purr, circling my hips. "I couldn't resist him. I knew he would fill me all the way up. Knew he would fuck me until I screamed."

"Has he done that?" Mrs. Green asks. "Made you scream?"

I pull my face into a bratty pout, rubbing my hard nipples side to side against Mr. Green's chest. "Not yet."

All this time, Mr. Green has been trying to be furtive about driving himself slowly up into my wet heat, but now his tether snaps. One second I'mstraddling his lap, the next I've been thrown onto my back on the couch and Mr. Green is no longer trying to keep the repeated pounds of his manhood into my body a secret. His hefty, muscular frame presses me down until I'm gasping for air, my thighs open and shaking, shaking, shaking with the powerof his entries. The living room fills with wet, squelching sounds of him entering my wet hole and he does nothing to quiet his loud grunts.

"Look at you." Mrs. Green shakes her head, but with my head thrown back, I can see her hand disappearing beneath her dress, the bliss that steams across her face. "You filthy man. Fucking that little girl because you can't help it. You better not come inside of her. You better not."

"I can't pull out. It's too sweet," he rasps, his thrusts quickening, so fast a scream begins to build in my throat, his oncoming peak colliding with mine. "Fuck. Christ. It's too late. I can't…fuuuuuuuck."

My scream is unleashed and it joins with Mr. Green's prolonged groan, the jerk of his flesh inside me and the never-ending flood of hot seed. He grinds down and curses, trying to wring himself dry inside me, and I pull hisbuttocks closer, sinking my nails into that flesh, encouraging him to overflowme. And when Mrs. Green's cries of pleasure join ours, it becomes too much again. I'm splintered apart by three unique free falls and I hit the bottom hard,Orangeness blanketing my vision.

Before I let sleep claim me, I watch Mr. and Mrs. Green share a laugh and a reassuring kiss above me. With their arms around one another, they look down at me with such fondness and care that I feel completely safe surrendering to the night.

CHAPTER FOUR
Mr. Red

It's a much different experience staying with the Greens. There is no tension the next morning when I wake up and venture from guest room to kitchen. No, there are banana walnut pancakes, a variety of syrup choices and tea. I sit at the kitchen table giggling at Mr. Green's locker room stories and Mrs. Green's tales from meditation class. It reminds me of being on the compound, except I'm not identified as merely someone's daughter here. I'm an adult. My own person.

I help Mrs. Green clean the dishes and watch as she slow dances with Mr. Green around the kitchen table, marrying the soap suds on their hands. There was happiness in this house yesterday, but today there is…abandon. They've done something risky bringing a third person into their sexual life, and I'm relieved to bear witness to it paying off.

I'm extremely attracted to Mr. Green—in a different way than I'm attracted to Mr. Orange. One man is warm and steady while the other is volatile as the ocean. But I love taking them into my body. I love that it is having a positive effect on their marriages and leaving them freer to express themselves. For example, Mr. Green's confidence could not be more rock solid as he dips his wife and lays a smack on her butt, walking toward me with a chuckle.

My fingers curl into my palm with the need to touch his big chest, but I suppress it and remain satisfied. I know where I want to stand with these families who have brought me into their homes and it revolves around trust. I will never overstep.

Mr. Green lays a kiss on my forehead, his expression turning serious. "You're going to Mr. and Mrs. Red's house this afternoon."

"Yes." I smile. "I'm…curious about them. I know almost nothing about them."

"You'll be safe, DOLLY. You can trust us on that," Mrs. Green says, trading a glance with her husband, and I sense instability in their energy. "But Mr. Red…he's a complicated man. Just remember you don't have to do anything that makes you uncomfortable."

I still have those words ringing in my ears an hour later when the limousine drops me off in front of the Red residence. It is by far the largest, most ornate home of all. Two Rolls Royces sit parked in the multi-car garage, a golf course spreads out on either side and around back. There is a chilly air to the home that the other two didn't have. My stomach churns along with the pebbles beneath my feet as I approach the front door, suitcase in hand.

The chimes go off inside when I ring the bell and a maid answers, taking my measure with a sweep of her cool eyes. "This way, if you please. Mrs. Red is expecting you in the salon."

I swallow hard and follow the stoic woman through a room decorated in multiple shades of grey. There isn't a single sound in the house, apart from the muffled ticking of a clock. Moments later, when I enter the salon, Mrs. Red rises from a chaise lounge, tucking blonde hair behind her ear. "DOLLY." She clears the rust from her voice. "You're even more beautiful than I remember."

"Thank you," I reply, feeling self-conscious. Especially when the maid takes my luggage and I have no idea what to do with my hands. "You have a lovely home."

Mrs. Red nods. "Won't you sit down? We have a lot to discuss." I cross the expensive rug and take a seat across from Mrs. Red on a velvet settee. "Well, how has the arrangement been treating you so far?"

"Very well," I say, crossing my ankles to match her. "Mrs. Red, I hope I'm not being too forward. But…is there a reason you're so nervous?"

Her smile remains frozen in place. "How can you tell?"

"It's something I can feel. I felt it the first time we met, too."

Apart from a crease between her arched brows, she shows no reaction to that. "Leave us, please," she directs at the maid, before returning her attention to me. "I'm afraid our situation is little different than the others. It's less about wanting to spice up a marriage or satisfy a man in his prime…and more about catering to a…taste. Yes, I suppose you could call it a taste."

"Okay," I say, smiling to encourage her. "Mr. Red is the one with the… taste?"

"Yes," she heaves on a breath, her fingers beginning to fidget.

It's too much for me to bear—her nerves and my increasing ones. I go down on my knees and walk toward Mrs. Red. Ignoring her increased alarm,

I pull some calm from down deep inside me and lay a hand on her forearm, letting it drift out of me and into her. Her eyes soften almost immediately, the rise and fall of her chest slowing to a regular pace. "Oh my. You're better than a Xanax."

I chuckle even though I have no idea what that is. "I was raised not to be judgmental, Mrs. Red. You can tell me anything you want."

Mrs. Red rolls her lips inward and sighs. "A few weeks ago, I went into Mr. Red's home office—" With an eye roll, she breaks off. "I'm getting ahead of myself. Mr. Red is a United States congressman, DOLLY. He's run uncontested for several terms, and well, he's a very prominent politician." She waves at the fireplace across the room where I see framed commendations and photos, although I'm too far away to notice the finer details. "You must be squeaky clean to remain in such a prestigious office forso long and…we are. He is. It's just that I went into his office and found a website open on his computer…"

"What kind of website?"

"Pornography," she breathes, her knee beginning to bounce. "It was the nature of the videos that surprised me so much. Stepfather punishes stepdaughter. Stepdaughter seduces stepfather. Stepdaddy acts naughty when wife goes to the store…" She trails off with a headshake. "I checked the history and he'd watched hundreds with similar titles. He'd been watching them for a very long time."

"So he…" A little ripple of heat between my thighs catches me off-guard. I know nothing of this kind of taste, as Mrs. Red puts it. Stepfathers aren't supposed to be intimate with their stepdaughters. That's not something that needs to be explained. That type of relationship would be wrong. So why is there a melting sensation in my middle? "So Mr. Red fantasizes about this. Do you have children or stepchildren?"

"No," she blurts. "God, no."

"And what is it you want from me?"

She regards me for a moment. "We have a good sex life for a couple that has been married as long as we have. I love him. He loves me. But this?" Her shoulders sag. "It's a turn off for me. I can't play along and call him Daddy—and I know, because I tried. It was a miserable failure."

"Daddy," I repeat, the word rolling off my tongue like summer lemonade. "That's what he likes to be called."

"Yes. That's the main root of it, to be perfectly frank. He wants to be Daddy." Her worry is obvious. "Is that a deal breaker for you?"

"No." No, I think…it might be the opposite, but I have to explore the bubble of excitement in my blood later. Right now, Mrs. Red needs to be reassured. "What do you want from me tonight?"

She's quiet for several beats. "We can't have him on these questionable porn sites. Information is hacked far too easily these days. I've already had a full wipe done on his computer. But now the satisfaction of his taste needs to come from somewhere. If he's going to slake these urges, it needs to happen in the privacy of our own home where he can't harm his career." A light smile transforms her face. "I've made peace with his needs and I'm looking forward to knowing he's being fulfilled, DOLLY. I want you to know I'm okay with this."

"Okay with what?" I whisper.

"My husband being your Daddy for the night."

That string of words almost knocks me backwards. A zip of eagerness races over my skin, but I'm still a touch unsettled. "Mrs. Orange receivedpeace of mind and, I think, the control she needs in her marriage. Mrs. Green fulfilled a fantasy. That's why I felt permitted to be with their husbands. It was only just for the men. What would you get out of tonight, Mrs. Red? There needs to be something, or I don't think I'll feel right about it."

Her face warms. "I really do like you, DOLLY." She sweeps the room in a glance. "I want to protect my comfortable life. It might sound shallow, but I like my friends, my possessions, the ease I've become accustomed to. I will do anything necessary to prevent myself from losing what I've built. Andyes, I did build it. I might come across as the frivolous wife, but I'm equally responsible for getting us here. I plan to keep us here, too." A beat passes. "If I'm being honest, I'm taking a little pleasure in making this arrangement. It's strategic and proactive and I'm looking forward to tomorrow when I'm not waiting for a shoe to drop."

The low hum of relaxation she projects with that final admission satisfies me that she's telling the truth. With that final piece of the puzzle fitted into place, I let myself sink into the adventure ahead. This one might excite me most of all.

CHAPTER FIVE

I wait in the pool house for evening to fall. Well, pool house is what Mrs. Red calls the bright, airy duplex overlooking the golf course on one side, an Olympic-sized swimming pool on the other. There are several rooms tochoose from and I end up crawling into a circular bed positively covered in throw pillows of every color. After a brief nap, I shower and dress in the clothing Mrs. Red provided, smoothing lotion over every inch of my body.

In doing so, I notice how sexual I feel. Every touch is sensual and meant to stimulate. I press my hips to the bathroom sink and massage lotion into my breasts, slowly grinding myself against the white porcelain. What will Mr. Red look like? Will he be surprised by my presence, or is he aware I'm coming? I like the unknown, though. I've surprised myself with my ability to adapt since leaving the compound and I'm beginning to think my mother wascorrect. It's possible there is something unique about me that benefits others.I want it to be true so badly. After enhancing the relationships of the Oranges and Greens, I want this to be my calling.

I want them to be my calling.

With hope in my heart, I turn off the bathroom light and look myself over one final time in the full-length bedroom mirror. I've never worn shorts like this. Thin, tight. They're more like underwear, leaving the underside of my butt cheeks showing, the seam riding up like a wedgie. They should be more uncomfortable, but the pressure on all my intimate parts makes me pulse all over. The crop top I've been given is loose and hangs from one shoulder, cutting off an inch below my breasts. I'm not sure if I'm supposed to wear a bra, but I leave it off at the last second, feeling daring. Feeling alive and needed.

The only lit up part of the house is the dining room and I cross the yard, entering through the back door, gasping at the size of the table. It could seat a hundred people. Mrs. Red stands at a gleaming sideboard on one end of the dimly lit room, uncorking a bottle of wine. Candles flicker as I walk toward her and she greets me with a nervous smile.

"Normally I wouldn't be doing this myself, but I've given the staff a night off." She pours wine into three glasses, one by one. "For obvious reasons." I'm about to respond when a door closes in the distance, the walls of the house seeming to rumble. "The man of the house is home," she says, taking a giant gulp of red liquid. "Here goes nothing."

I'm unprepared for the gravity of Mr. Red. His aura invades the dining room before he does, vacillating between gold and orange. Intelligent, fierce, charismatic. And oh so handsome. Mr. Red is older than the other men by more than a few years, his whole head covered in thick, gray hair. He's not a man who has let his body age, though. This is a man who spends hours keeping himself fit. Everything about his energy tells me what I need to knowabout his personality. He brooks no disrespect, commands a room...and I know his secret.

I am his secret now.

When Mr. Red sees me, he slows to a stop, impatient fingers pausing in the process of loosening his tie. Obviously he does not expect to find a scantily clad young woman in his home and thus, he can't keep his reaction entirely schooled. Sharp eyes lose their edge and he makes a jagged sound. "Who is this?"

For all her nerves, Mrs. Red now seems almost aloof, casually sipping her wine. "This is DOLLY, dear. She's staying for dinner...and for the night." Mrs.Red gives me a meaningful look. "No chef tonight, so I'm going to go check on dinner. I'll be back in a few minutes. You two get acquainted."

On the way out of the room, Mrs. Red stops and whispers into herhusband's ear. He shows no reaction to whatever she says, but his disbelief reaches me where I stand. As his wife vanishes into the kitchen, his shock gives way to desire. So much of it that I have to press my thighs together. I expect him to approach me, to touch me, but he doesn't. No, he simply takes his seat at the head of the table, gesturing to the setting to his left. "Sit."

"Yes," I respond on autopilot, every cell in my body thrilling to that single, bitten off command. His fists rest on the table as I sway toward my seat and fall into it like a bored teenager, although I'm the furthest thing frombored. I'm alive.

Mrs. Red reenters the room carrying a covered pot. She sets it down in the middle of the table and ladles what appears to be pumpkin soup into our bowls. "I thought something light tonight would be just the thing," shebreezes, taking her seat. "Everybody dig in."

I reach for my spoon and stop, crossing my arms over my bare midriff. "I'm not hungry."

I feel, rather than see, Mr. Red's jaw flex. "Eat your dinner, young lady."

Wetness rushes between my thighs and I shift in my seat, trying to keep myself from reacting in earnest. "I said, I'm not hungry."

Across the table, Mrs. Red takes a spoonful of soup, her expression one of fascination. As if she can't believe how quickly and easily this is happening. I can't really believe it, either. This role has somehow settled over me like a second skin.

"Do you need to be fed like a child?" Mr. Red snaps, unbuttoning one of his sleeves and rolling it up to his elbow. "So be it. Get over here now."

My legs are shaking so violently, I almost can't stand up, but my eagerness to find out what's coming forces me up and around the table. I stop in front of Mr. Red with an eye roll and give him my back. Without facing him, I know his eyes are blazing a hot path up my thighs and barely covered bottom. I bite back a whimper when he grips my hips and jerks me down into his lap.

I'm still reeling over the rampant erection now wedged between the cheeks of my backside when Mr. Red scoots us closer to the table. "Open your spoiled little mouth," he whispers in my ear. "Or later tonight when everyone is sleeping, I'll make you open it for a lot more than soup."

Underneath the table, Mr. Red's thighs open wide, wider, until mine are draped over his muscular legs, leaving my core exposed. I send him a glare over my shoulder and feel his erection swell larger. "Fine."

His left hand takes hold of my jaw, applying pressure until my mouth pops open. Before I know what's happening, he guides a spoonful of soup between my lips. "Swallow," he orders gruffly into my hair. When I comply, he brings me another bite. "Again."

Briefly, I let my attention drift to Mrs. Red and find her looking oblivious, concerned only with her meal. As if she has no idea what's happening beneath the table. Or that I'm sitting in such a provocative position, her husband's rod of hard flesh pulsing in the split of my backside. And now he's setting the spoon down, moving his left hand beneath the table and cupping my sex.

"Shhh," he breathes into my hair. "Daddy had a hard day at work."

Two thick finger pads find my clit through the thin material of my shorts and begin circling it slowly. In seconds, I'm rattling the bars of a mental cage, trying not to scream and work my bottom on Mr. Red's lap…when he casually spoons a bite of soup into his mouth with his right hand. As if what's happening beneath the table is a secret only we know about. The wrongness of it somehow revs my need higher, hotter and my vision grows hazy, lust climbing my throat like ivy.

I can't have an orgasm like this, can I?

Right here at the table?

Mr. Red shows no signs of relenting. No, his fingers move faster and faster until I have no control over my own hips. I'm rubbing my bottom side to side and accepting his low grunts like a beggar gobbling up breadcrumbs. It's going to happen. I'm going to climax right here on his lap while he eats soup. Just as I'm about to capsize under the weight of my pleasure, Mr. Red stops touching me, resting his left hand on my thigh and squeezing firmly.

"Next time, do as you're told without the attitude, young lady," he enunciates as I try not to be obvious that I'm about to hyperventilate. Or cry. Or both. "I don't tolerate disrespect under my roof. Now tell your mother thank you for dinner and go wait in your room. We're going to have one of our talks tonight."

Moments later, I feel like I'm trapped in a dream as I stumble blindly across the backyard. I'm on fire. Every inch of my skin is branded and hotand needy. I'm so needy for Mr. Red. My nipples are in spikes and I can't stand the feeling of material chafing them, so I strip the shirt off as soon as I'm in the pool house. I stomp like a punished teenager to my room and slam the door shut, screaming through clenched teeth. I want to touch myself, but Idon't. I don't dare. Somehow I know I'll be in even worse agony if I take away this terrible edge he's given me.

I'm lying on my side on the bed, still panting with thwarted need, when the bedroom door opens and closes. Stubbornly, I refuse to turn around and Mr. Red sighs. "I'm not sure how your father disciplined you, young lady,but I'm the man in your life now. I'm your new father. I make the rules and itwill make my life much easier if you learn to obey them." His weight makes the bed dip and my stomach follows suit. "Don't you want to make Daddy's life easier?"

I don't answer. I can't. That word causes an uprising in my hormones.

"These shorts tell me the answer is yes." His hand coasts over my bottom, squeezing and releasing my cheeks rhythmically. "These shorts tell me you want to be the solution to all of my problems at the end of a hard day. Isn't that why you maneuver me into having our nightly talks?"

The mattress shifts and his body heat licks my back. I want him to roll me over and devour me, but I'm imbued with the stubbornness of the part I'm playing. A part that doesn't feel like a part at all. It feels real.

"Very well, DOLLY. If you're not going to speak with me like a big girl, I'll take what I need to relax and go back to the house." Mr. Red's weight leaves the bed. The lamp I turned on when I walked into the room is switched off, leaving nothing but the moonlight to illuminate the room. Behind me, I hear the faint sound of buttons being pulled through holes and a belt being unhooked, a zipper coming down. Anticipation makes me breathless and I'm wondering about Mr. Red's next move when he snatches my ankle and yanks me to the edge of the bed. "Get over here, brat." I whimper and start to struggle on instinct when my panties are ripped from my body. "All I want from my little princess is some appreciation when I get home. You're going to show me some right now, goddammit."

"I appreciate you," I blurt, damp pressure forming behind my eyes. "I'm sorry. I didn't mean to have an attitude."

Mr. Red tilts my chin up. "Why do you give me one?"

"I know it's wrong to want you," I whisper, reaching out to lower Mr. Red's pants, followed by the band of his briefs. His erection bobs out, proud and thick and long. "I know it's wrong to…hate sharing you."

His jaw loosens and sags when I begin to stroke him with two hands, watching him contritely through my eyelashes. "There's my good girl. I knew she was in there somewhere." He taps my right cheek. "Open up and show Daddy how sorry you are about his hard day."

I'm dying to taste Mr. Red that I don't bother with licking or teasing. No, my blood hums with the knowledge of what he needs. He's been waiting for this night for a long time. Thousands of fantasies have led to this. To me. So I devour him, grateful and enthusiastic, pulling on him with tight sucks and sliding him down my throat. Over and over, while he groans and fucks my mouth, hips cinching forward and back.

"That sweet, little mouth is a powerful thing, isn't it, young lady? Pissing me off one minute and making me a god the next." He threads his fingers through my hair, pressing and holding his manhood deep, deep, until I make a choking sound. "What a special treat it is for your Daddy, knowing it's waiting for him every night in the pool house." He pulls free of my mouth and strokes himself for me in a tight fist, leaving a drop of semen on the tip of my waiting tongue. "Mmmm. Good girl. We both know what my greatest treasure is, though. Daddy couldn't keep his hands off it at dinner, could he?"

I'm so wet for Mr. Red that the insides of my thighs are slick. I'm fondling my own breasts, my sobs punctuating the air. "I wanted you to make me come in front of her, Daddy. Why didn't you?"

At my first utterance of the title, Mr. Red seems to expand, his chest and shoulders gaining even more strength. His energy pulses. Pulses with a sense of homecoming. "I wanted to satisfy that little pussy, too…" He pulls me to my feet and kisses my mouth thoroughly, tonguing me until I run out of air. Slowly, he turns me around and pushes me facedown over the bed, leaving me balanced on my forearms, my bottom in the air. "I always want to satisfy you, little girl, but she's starting to get suspicious. You and Daddy have been having too many talks lately." He smacks his hard erection against my backside a few times. "I have to stop myself from coming home on lunch breaks just to have a stern talk with tight, little DOLLY."

"I'd be waiting for you, Daddy."

Mr. Red plugs my entrance with the tip of his length, then sinks all the way in with a long, ragged groan. "Oh, Jesus fucking Christ."

I'm already vibrating with the approach of my climax. He's filling every inch of me and I'm still keyed up from the way he touched me at dinner. One thrust and I'm going to erupt. His energy is so bold and debauched and wild, it's heightening my experience, connecting us even more than I already feel we are. I turn my head to the right and moan at our reflection in the window. Old on young. A powerful man and his secret. "Am I tight enough for you, Daddy?"

A shudder moves through Mr. Red and he rears back, driving into me with a grunt. "Never felt anything like it. My God. I can barely get in and out."

One more thrust and my walls clench, clench, tightening to the point of agony before release finds me. Finally. I work myself shamelessly on Mr. Red's thick arousal, grinding my clit anywhere it can find friction, prolonging my orgasm. "Daddy. Daddy."

"Son of a bitch," he breathes, pressing his front to my back and fucking me in a frenzy. His testicles swing up and smack me repeatedly between the thighs, his breath rasping into the curve of my neck. "No one can ever know about this, young lady. No one can know I'm obsessed with your pretty, little cunt. Do you hear me? Daddy will give you everything you ever want if you just keep our secret. Especially from your mother."

"I won't tell," I whimper, reaching back to spread my cheeks wide for Daddy to look at. "I just want to be your good girl forever."

Mr. Red flattens me on the bed with a roar, slamming his manhood into me with great, punishing drives, knocking the breath out of my lungs. Making me scream into the mattress. And when he bears down and comes with a mighty shudder, I join him in my second climax. There's no way to avoid it when such overwhelming completion wraps around him. It encompasses me. Makes me proud. This experience Mr. Red has wanted forever has finally happened and there's no mistaking his awe.

Or his growing hunger to do it again. Soon.

I smile at him when he falls to his side on the bed, red faced andbreathing heavily. Still playing the good girl, I curl my fists against his cheek and snuggle close. "You better get back soon, Daddy," I whisper, kissing his mouth and letting my tongue mate gently with his. "We can't get caught."

A little while later, I'm sitting in the backyard under the stars when a light goes on upstairs. It's the master bedroom. I watch drowsily as Mr. Red walks into the bedroom, greeted by Mrs. Red. They smile at one another andembrace for long minutes, an obviously cathartic moment taking place. Insidemy chest, I feel my heart flutter and expand with knowledge.

The knowledge that I've found my purpose in Los Angeles.

EPILOGUE

One year later

Iᴛ's ɢɪʀʟs' ɴɪɢʜᴛ out.

I smile as I climb out of the limousine and shoulder my overnight bag. As usual, the chauffer was sent to pick me up at my apartment in Beverly Hills, taking me to the Orange residence. I've been living in my gorgeous penthouse for some time now. After my first three magical nights with the couples, Mrs. Orange got in touch with the best realtor in Los Angeles and each couple contributed funds to buy me the penthouse. I couldn't believe their generosity. I still can't.

I'm living a fairy tale.

Every Sunday night, Mrs. Red calls me with the weekly schedule. A calendar organized into which husband I'll "sit" for on what nights. I like how it constantly changes. Sometimes Mr. Orange needs me more than usual, because Mrs. Orange is out of town. Those weeks, I'm usually thrown up against the door as I soon as I walk inside, my ripped panties pressed to his nose while he takes me in a fury, whether or not the maids are watching. Sometimes I think he even prefers having them observe. Yes, Mr. Orange is definitely my most arrogant lover.

Mr. and Mrs. Green like their visits more spaced out. Sometimes Mrs. Greenlikes to catch us in an upscale hotel room. Or in the backseat of Mr. Green's car, fogging up the windows in the Hollywood Hills. Other times, she just likes me to spend the night between them in their bed, watching with a smile on her face and busy fingers between her legs as I ride Mr. Green and tell him how magnificent he is—and I'm never lying.

Mr. Red is my Daddy. I save a little something special inside me for him, even though I love all of the husbands equally. My favorite is whomever I'm with. Still, I pulse all over thinking of Mr. Red relieving his stress during one of our little "talks." The rigid man I met that first night has learned to smile more. His relationship with Mrs. Red has visibly improved and she's started participating more in the game. Just last week, she told Mr. Red I needed swimming lessons and suggested he teach me. He brought home several swimsuits for me to try on. While Mrs. Red waited outside the bathroom, he came inside to help me tie the itty bitty top and he took me against the bathroom sink while reassuring his wife through the door that we'd be right out.

I stop outside the front door of the Orange residence and press a hand to my flaming cheeks. One year and this arrangement has not only shown zero signs of losing its incredible shine, its perfection seems to be enhanced with every visit. I'm in love with love, even more than I always was, because I'm now in deep, enduring love with six individuals. The wives, the husbands. And they love me back.

There are two free nights per week that I spend on my own, walking the bright, boisterous streets of Los Angeles, letting the emotions of those around me catch and take hold. I learn through walking in the shoes of others and I bring those experiences to my relationships with the Oranges, Greens and Reds.

Someday I'll visit the compound and tell my parents about the marriages I've become an integral part of. My lips twitch. I'm just not sure when I'll be able to fit a vacation into my very demanding schedule. I've just had two nights off in a row and the energy pouring from the house tells me I've been missed.

Before I can even knock, the door swings open and not one, not two, but three husbands fill the doorway. Girls' night out is a rarity, but when it rolls around, I husband sit for all three men while the wives go out on the town.

I have to admit, it's better than any holiday. Even if the excess of testosterone and lust usually causes me to Orange out afterward. Worth it.

Mr. Green snags my wrist and drags me inside, up against his impressive body. While his mouth works over mine in a passionate kiss, Mr. Orange crowds me from behind, moaning into my hair and grinding his erection against my backside. As always, Mr. Red stands to the side with a glass of whiskey in his hand and waits for me to acknowledge him separately. And I do. As soon as Mr. Green lets me come up for air, I flutter my eyelashes at Mr. Red. "Hi, Daddy," I mouth, for his eyes alone.

His cheek ticks in response. Then he winks.

I'm spun around to encounter a rough, demanding kiss from Mr. Orange. He guides my hand to his erection, urging me to stroke him off without words. Cool air glides over my buttocks and I sense my skirt has been dragged down. That theory is confirmed when I hear Mr. Green's knees hit the floor and feel his tongue dragging up the center of my bottom.

"Good Lord," Mrs. Green singsongs as she enters the room. "They can't even wait until we get out the door."

Mrs. Orange snorts. "Don't mind us, gentlemen."

Mr. Orange breaks the kiss, his mouth twisting in a smirk. And then Mr. Red steps into his place, leaning in to whisper in my ear. "Whatever happens tonight, just remember that I'm allowing it, young lady."

Knowing what this man—what *all* of these men need—to be satisfied, I nod dutifully. "Thank you, Daddy," I mouth. "I love you."

He reaches around to squeeze and give a light slap to my backside; which Mr. Green is still hard at work on with his wicked tongue. "Good girl."

The front door opens, and I wave goodbye to the laughing wives in a daze, security and love surrounding me like a heat wave. Then I'm too lost in sensation to think. I'm carried to a bedroom and feasted on for hours by my three men, their growls of rapture echoing off the walls of the house. Later, they hold me close and kiss every inch of my fevered skin like I belong to them.

I do. I'll belong to them forever.

Their devoted husband sitter.

THE END

CPSIA information can be obtained
at www.ICGtesting.com
Printed in the USA
BVHW011752150321
602550BV00009B/857